Once Upon a Kiss

A Novella

Ashley I. Hansen

Chapter 1

The icy glass of the bus window felt good as I pressed my face against it. Right before my eyes, the streets of Brussels were flying by. I couldn't help but pinch myself. Nana had shown me so many pictures of where she'd grown up and now I, Rosie Jacobs, was in Brussels. After so many years of dreaming about it, I was here. Thinking of Nana, my eyes watered a bit, but I ignored it. I wouldn't cry—not here in Belgium. Not in Nana's homeland. A country filled with magic, as Nana would say.

"Ring around the *Rosie...*" An obnoxious voice whispered in my ear. "Ding dong, is anybody home?"

I smacked the hand that incessantly tapped my shoulder. "Knock it off, Jeremey."

Jeremey, dark haired and gangly, snorted with laughter as he dodged another well aimed smack, I sent his way. He hurried to his seat before Madame Thomas could catch him out of it. His friend Nathan gave him a high five as he sat down. I barely contained an eye roll.

"Boys are so weird," Olive said, brushing her long dark hair behind her ears

"Yep." I nodded in agreement.

"At least they notice you." She sighed as she turned her attention back to her book.

I shook my head. At that very moment, Nathan was staring at her like she was a puzzle he couldn't figure out. Maybe I should tell Olive or maybe I should tell Nathan to get the courage to talk to her. I turned my attention back to the window as Brussels passed by. Perhaps Nana had traveled down this very street. Maybe she had stopped at that shop to pick up a loaf of freshly baked bread. Maybe that was the streetlight she had met Papa under.

"May I have your attention everyone." Madame Thomas's voice cut through my thoughts "We will be arriving at the castle shortly. Make sure you have your sketch books ready and do try to speak only French when we are there. That counts towards your overall grade."

Several students groaned, but I didn't mind. I'd learned how to speak French from Nana. I could speak it fluently, but when it came to writing in French I was abysmal. Nana used to cluck her tongue at my atrocious French spelling.

"*C'est tragique,*" she would say dramatically before giving me a wink.

I bumped into the seat in front of me as the

bus stopped abruptly. I righted myself and hurried to grab my sketch book. I was a terrible artist no matter how hard I tried. As the doors of the bus opened, there was a mad rush of students as we all tried to exit. As soon as I stepped down, my breath was taken away by the beautiful gardens surrounding the castle.

"We have our tour in one hour," Madame Thomas called. "Don't be late. They've graciously given you all permission to look at the gardens in the meantime. Don't trample the flowers. If you do, you'll automatically get a failing grade."

Olive gave me a horrified look.

"Oh, don't worry about it. You wouldn't dream of trampling flowers."

"But what if I do on accident?" she squeaked. "I don't want to get a bad grade. That'll ruin my four-year plan. Then we won't be able to go to college together."

"We're going to the same college?"

She nodded.

"You won't trample any flowers. Come on," I told her, trying to hide a smile.

She shook her head. "I think I'll stay right here."

My shoulder sagged a little. I had no desire to wander the gardens by myself. From the corner of my eye, I caught Jeremey staring at me. As our eyes met, he gave me a mischievous smile and started walking towards me. On second thought, I couldn't stand any more of Jeremey's nagging.

"I'll see you in an hour," I told Olive before sprinting off.

I heard Madame Thomas yell at me to slow down and I nearly did, but when I looked behind me, Jeremey was giving chase. I wanted to scream. How childish could he be? I sped up and rushed around a corner, making sure to stay on the trails. I could still hear his pounding feet behind me. In a move that would have impressed any movie stunt double, I leaped over one flower garden and landed on the next path. I ducked quickly behind a tree, trying not to breathe loudly.

Jeremey ran past and I felt like doing a victory cry. At the thought, my face burned. Who was the childish one now? I was fifteen years old; I shouldn't be running away from boys, no matter how annoying I found them. It's not like I thought they had cooties like I did when I was six.

I pressed my face close to the tree, breathing in its smell as my heart rate slowed. Eventually, I turned around. I had jumped off the path to hide behind the tree. Just beyond the tree was a moat.

I couldn't help but smile. It really was just like a fairytale castle with a moat. Maybe there were some scary beasts lurking in the moat, keeping invaders at bay. I bit back a giggle. That was something Nana would have said. I edged towards the water and sat near it. Staring into it, it looked calm —not a moat monster in sight.

RIBBIT

I nearly squealed at the loud sound and just

caught myself from tumbling into the water.

RIBBIT

I looked around and saw a frog bigger than my hand perched near my knee. The giggle that I had bit back burst out of me.

"I suppose you're a cursed prince?"

RIBBIT.

"Should I kiss you and break your spell then? I'm not a princess, but who knows? Maybe I had a great-great-great grandmother who was."

The frog didn't make a sound. Instead it just stared at me with unblinking eyes. Maybe I should kiss it. Why not kiss it? Nana would have done it. She would have called it an adventure.

I shrugged my shoulders. "Well, here goes nothing."

I leaned down. The frog didn't move. I pursed my lips. The frog didn't move. I placed my lips on its slimy head and gave it my very first kiss. My lips tingled with a warm sensation as I pulled away. The frog was still a frog. I felt slightly disappointed.

"Well, I tried," I told the frog as I wiped my lips. "I should get back though. I don't want to be late or Madame Thomas might have steam pour out her ears."

I stood to leave, brushing dirt off of my pants, but then something very odd happened. There was a loud pop that rattled the ground, causing me to fall. A brilliant flash of light lit the already sunny sky. I covered my eyes. Within moments, the ground had stopped shaking.

"My true love, I do thank thee," a deep voice said in heavily accented English. Before I could look to see who it was, I was pulled up from the ground.

I dropped my hands from my eyes and got a glimpse of an extremely handsome boy before he pressed his lips against mine. I instantly became dazed. This was my first real kiss and it was delightful, as Nana would say. Wait…I shouldn't have been thinking about Nana while I was having my first kiss. Wait…I'd already had my first kiss with the frog. Wait…who was kissing me?

I pushed the stranger away.

"I do apologize, my dear lady. I was simply glad you'd finally came," he said, looking down at me adoringly. "I've waited so long for my true love."

He was at least two heads taller than me, with golden hair and muscles that made him look like he grew up training for the Olympics. But his face was young. He couldn't be much older than me. His clothing looked like it came straight from a Renaissance fair.

"I'm sorry, who are you?"

He bowed deeply and kissed my hand, causing me goose pimples. "I am Prince Sebastián III of Geníru."

"Oh…." I replied, baffled. "And why do you think I'm your one true love?"

Why was I even asking him that? Why did it even matter? That kiss…. well, as far as real first kisses went, I'm sure it was the best one in the entire history of the world. I wouldn't mind if he kissed me again. Who cared if he might be a little crazy? Maybe he really was a prince.

"You broke my curse." He smiled brightly, showing perfectly white, straight teeth. "As you can see my, dear lady, I am no longer a frog."

My heart stopped pounding and I looked around. The frog was indeed gone and Prince Sebastián III of Geníru was standing right where the frog had been.

Chapter 2

"Rosie?" Olive called, shaking me out of my shock. "Rosie, where are you?"

Prince Sebastián cocked his head in the direction of Olive's voice and said, "Your name is Rosie? What a beautiful name for a beautiful maiden and my one true love."

I placed my hand over his mouth. "Please be quiet."

He gently removed my hand from his mouth and kissed it. "Anything for you, my love."

Irritation flashed through me and I yanked my hand away from him.

"We don't even know each other. I could be annoying or a slob or a million other things that drive you crazy."

"One thing you say is true. I am crazy for you," he replied.

"But you don't know me," I reiterated.

"You broke the curse. Therefore, you are my

one true love. Only true love's kiss can break a curse."

My head spun. That was usually how spells were broken in the fairytales Nana read to me growing up. I began to run through a list of fairytales in my head. Snow White had met her prince how many times before they lived happily ever after? Oh, once. She couldn't have known him well. Cinderella had danced with her prince at the ball, but did they really know each other after one dance? Sleeping Beauty…had she even met him before he kissed her and broke her curse?

I looked up at Sebastián. His eyes reminded me of the look my dog gave me every time I got home from school. Puppy love. Gross…but that kiss hadn't been gross.

"Rosie, there you are," Olive said as she gingerly made her way around the gardens towards us. "Who's your friend?"

Sebastián bowed to her and spoke before I could stop him. "I am Prince Sebastián III of Geníru. And you must hail from an exotic part of the world."

My face went beet red. Olive did look exotic. She was oddly fascinated with genealogy and found out she had ancestors from Gabon, Switzerland, Hawaii, Ireland, and a few other places I couldn't remember. She even had Cherokee ancestors.

Olive gave a lopsided smile. "If you call Wisconsin exotic then I suppose so."

"Wisconsin? I do not believe I know where this is," he replied, tapping his chin in confusion.

"It's one of the many states in the United States of America. Which I guess makes me exotic—you know, melting pot and all. Or tossed salad, whatever you prefer to call it."

"The United States of America…" He trailed off, looking at her like she was telling a big joke.

"It's located in North America. In French it's pronounced *États-Unis d'Amérique*," Olive said with a perfect French accent.

"Ah, North America. I have never heard of *États-Unis d'Amérique* or the United States. It must be a small country."

Olive opened her mouth to respond but a shrill whistle blew. Sebastián covered his ears.

"Oh, I completely forgot. They cancelled our tour. Madame Thomas is awfully upset and wants to leave." Olive grabbed my arm and began to pull me away from Sebastián.

Sebastián followed behind me. We made it to the bus in record time. When Jeremey caught sight of Sebastián, he glared daggers at him. Maybe having Sebastián around wouldn't be all bad—plus, he did kiss really well. My face began to go red again. I was such a ninny. That's the word Nana would have used. I began to climb the stairs of the bus behind Olive.

"Young man, you are not part of my class," Madame Thomas said, putting her arm out to stop Sebastián.

"But…" he began, flustered.

I jumped down the steps to him and whispered in his ear, "You're free now. Go live a wonderful life in Geníru."

I hopped back up the stairs before he could stop me. The doors closed, blocking his entrance. I sat down beside Olive and sighed. What an odd adventure I'd had. I was glad to be rid of Sebastián. He was a bit annoying.

The bus began to move and I glanced out the window. Sebastián was gone. I shrugged. Good riddance.

"Who was that boy?" Olive looked up from the book she had instantly shoved her nose into when she sat down. "Was he an actor? He was very good. He even knew the name of a country that hasn't existed for about three hundred years. Geníru is now a part of France. Has been since 1750."

"That can't be right. He is from Geníru."

"He must have been teasing you. He was probably acting the part of the long-lost Prince of Geníru. Maybe he's in a play? I wonder if someone wrote a musical about Geníru? I'd love to see it if they have."

Chapter 3

The world seemed to spin around me as I tried to process what Olive was saying. My heartbeat pounded in my ears, making it hard to concentrate. If Geníru really hadn't existed for three hundred years, how long had Sebastián been a frog?

"When did this long-lost prince disappear? Before or after Geníru was defeated by France?"

"Well, they weren't really defeated by France. France had a legitimate claim—"

"Olive!" I broke in.

"Oops, I went all history professor again, didn't I?"

I nodded. "Now, when did this prince disappear?"

"A good thirty years before Geníru became part of France. No one is exactly sure of the date either. It's all very mysterious and tragic. Something that could be straight out of a fairytale. He actually disappeared somewhere in this region. Even more mysterious is that no one is exactly sure where the Geníru Castle is anymore. It's like it vanished into thin air or was gobbled up by history. I would love to find it."

I could feel all the blood drain out of my face. Sebastián had been a frog for more than three hundred years and I had just let him loose on his own in the twenty-first century! What if he tried to duel someone or something crazy like that?

"Rosie." Olive shook me.

"Yeah?"

"What's wrong? You look like you saw a ghost."

"Do the history books give this prince a name?" I asked, feeling small.

"No. No one in Geníru was allowed to speak of the prince after he disappeared and his name was blotted out of documents. All very dramatic, I think."

I looked out the window, not really seeing any of the beauty that we passed by. A name didn't really prove anything. I had kissed a frog and it had turned into an actual prince. A prince from a different century, but a prince nonetheless. I began to have an awful feeling in my gut. Poor Sebastián. He had been a frog for so long, then I'd come along kissed him and abandoned him in a strange time period he knew nothing about.

"Rosie, are you sick? You don't look well."

"I'm fine."

"You're lying, Rosie Jacobs. I've known you since I was four and every time you lie you scrunch up your nose. You better stop. It'll make you get wrinkles."

"Hey," I protested.

Olive shrugged. "Well, it's true. Now, tell me what's wrong or I'll tell Madame Thomas you're sick."

I groaned. Olive could be so stubborn sometimes—well, actually all the time. It was one of the things I loved about her, but at this moment I wished she would just let it go.

"Fine, but you can't say I'm crazy."

"I won't," Olive affirmed.

"When we got to the castle, I ran off to get away from Jeremey."

"His teasing is getting out of hand," Olive put in.

"Right. Anyway, I ran towards the moat and hid from him. That's when I spotted the frog."

"Let me guess—you picked the frog up and kissed it?" Olive interrupted me once more. "But it didn't turn into a handsome prince. Where does that actor guy come into the story?"

"Do you want me to tell you or not?"

"Sorry," Olive said, her face turning red.

"I did kiss the frog." I paused. "Nothing happened for a moment, but then there was a loud noise and the ground starting shaking. There was a flash of light and then Sebastián was there and he kissed me."

Olive's mouth dropped open but she didn't interrupt.

"It was…well, never mind how the kiss was. That's not important. Then he introduced himself as Prince Sebastián III of Geníru and he started spouting off how I was his one true love. Yada yada yada."

Olive blinked once, slowly. "It must have been a trick or prank or something."

"How, Olive? No one knew I was going to go over there. I didn't even know. Who would have placed a frog in that exact location and waited for some silly girl to find it and then kiss it all for an elaborate prank? How could they have even planned that?"

"Good point," she responded. "It's just so hard to believe."

"But it happened and now I've left a long-lost prince from the eighteenth century alone in the twenty-first century."

∞∞∞

"Tell me again exactly what happened after you kissed the frog?" Olive asked.

I sighed. "Olive, we've been over this a thousand times already."

"I know, I just don't want to miss anything. It could be important."

Miraculously, the bus came to a stop, ending

her nonstop questions. I grabbed my bag and headed for the exit.

"We'll have to go back and find him somehow," Olive said, following me.

I stopped, nearly causing her to run over me. "How are we supposed to do that? We aren't allowed to go anywhere without Madame Thomas."

"We'll have to sneak out of our room tonight."

"Olive, I can't believe that just came out of your mouth."

She smiled. "I suppose my rebellious teen side is finally kicking in. Won't my parents be proud?"

I tried to hide my laughter as we exited the bus. A quaint inn lay ahead of us. It looked like it belonged in a storybook. I had to pinch myself to make sure I wasn't dreaming. After all, I had kissed a frog today that turned into a prince.

"Rosie, I found you!"

I spun around. Prince Sebastián III of Geníru in all his eighteenth-century glory was striding towards me.

Chapter 4

I 'd thought I'd lost you forever," He proclaimed, taking my hands in his.

My tongue seemed to be glued to the top of my mouth.

Olive recovered before I did. She grabbed us both and dragged us around the corner and out of view of Madame Thomas.

"Can I call you Sebastián?" she asked.

Sebastián opened his mouth to respond, but she cut him off.

"It doesn't matter. I'm going to call you Sebastián. We can't very well be calling you Prince Sebastián III. Everyone would think we were crazy or part of an acting group."

"What does the maiden mean?" he asked me as he leaned confidently against the wall.

I took a deep breath. "What year is it?"

"1718."

"Are you sure?"

"Of course, dear lady."

I looked over at Olive.

"You need to tell him," she whispered.

"Tell me what? Was the wedding canceled?"

"Whose wedding?" I asked.

"Rosie!" Olive snapped. "Quit stalling."

"Right. Well, there is no easy way to tell you this." I said, turning to look Sebastián in the face. "The current year is 2020."

"You jest, dear lady," he said, smiling fondly at me, but something in his eyes told me he didn't feel as confident as his words sounded.

"I don't jest and you have to stop calling me lady. It's not normal to call people that nowadays."

The smile on Sebastián's face faded as he looked between Olive and me, noticing for the first time how we were dressed.

"This is not a jest? This isn't one of Cousin Albert's games?"

"Would your cousin Albert really put in this much effort to trick you? I mean, look around. Doesn't everything look vastly different?" I asked.

He tilted his head. "I did ride in a marvelous carriage that drove itself. That's how I found you. I jumped into the carriage and cried 'follow that large carriage' and the driver did. He had the audacity to ask for money when he dropped me off. I was in too much of a hurry to catch you so I gave him a few gold coins."

"Everything he just said belongs in a novel," Olive responded slowly. "This is madness."

"Just like Albert." Sebastián shrugged. "Madness is everywhere. It's not something we discuss."

Was his family line full of mad kings or something? I put my hand to my forehead. He didn't seem to be taking any of this seriously.

"Sebastián, who placed the curse on you?" I asked. "And did they say how long it would last?"

"Katarina. I told Albert we should not take it but he never listens to me."

"How long did she say you'd be cursed?" I interrupted him.

"Until my true love found me…and…" Realization seemed to finally hit him. It looked like he'd taken a punch to the gut. "She said if my true love never found me, I'd be a frog till the end of time."

He pushed himself off the wall and began to pace. Olive and I remained silent. I watched him pace three steps one way, then three steps back. Over and over and over again. I began to wonder how many people had kissed him as a frog. Was I the only one?

He stopped. "If I've been a frog for three hundred years, all of my family is dead. Everyone I've ever known is dead."

My throat felt dry, but I nodded.

"What happened to Geníru?"

I looked at Olive. She shook her head. Her face looked glum and bleak. I looked back at Sebastián, his eyes pleading.

"What happened?" he asked again.

"It's no longer a country. It's now part of

France," I whispered, afraid to speak any louder.

He stumbled back against the wall and slumped down it.

"Our worst enemy took over my country." he stated, clenching his hands into fists. "This is all Albert's fault. The next time I see him…."

His words faded. It was the worst thing to watch and I sat down next to him, placing one of my hands on top of a clenched fist.

"I'm really sorry. I can't say I understand how you feel because I don't. I wish I could help you change the past but I can't. But I can help you navigate today's world."

His eyes locked on mine and he smiled but it was a sad smile. "I would appreciate that, but first we have to go back to Geníru."

"We? As in both of us?"

He nodded. "The curse isn't fully broken. I have to return the amulet to the throne room before two midnights pass."

"None of that exists anymore, and why do you need to take an amulet back?"

"It's part of the curse. If we don't return it, both of us will die."

Chapter 5

My mouth hung open like a broken door and my brain spun around, searching for words, but all I could think of was what would Nana say in a situation like this?

"Oh fiddlesticks!" I cried, the words tumbling out of my mouth before I could stop them.

"I beg your pardon, dear Rosie, I don't understand."

"None of us understand Rosie's old-fashioned talk—well, I guess to you it would be future-fashioned talk." Olive tapped her chin then shook her head. "Never mind that, what do you mean you will both die if you don't return the amulet?"

"'Twas cousin Albert's idea," Sebastián began. "Of course, Katarina found out. She knows everything. She tried to warn me of the consequences. They say she could see the future—even predict her own death."

I shook my head, trying to clear my thoughts.

"Maybe you could start from the beginning."

"Katarina was a witch who lived in Geníru. She was old. Older than the ancient forest but you'd never be able to tell. Her face had no wrinkles and she looked as young as us, but if you looked at her eyes you could see the time in them."

"Can I just ask one question? How did you know she was old?" Olive asked, looking intrigued.

"Olive!" I snapped.

"Right. Sorry, continue."

Sebastián looked at Olive. "We knew because she'd always been known to the royal court. There had always been a record of her. My great-grandfather would tell me stories of her when I was just a boy."

I shivered. I'd never been fond of such stories.   "For the most part she was harmless. She would give herbs of healing to people who were sick. People would come from miles around to ask her what their future held and she would tell them."

"Where do you come into this story?" I interrupted.

"She had a Ruby Amulet. That's where her power came from. It's how she stayed young. Albert thought if we stole it, we could use it to protect Geníru. We are—were—a small country. The French were constantly trying to take over our land. Albert had me convinced it would work. I shouldn't have believed him. Katarina could see my future. She knew what would happen.

"I went to her, pretending to want to know my future. She told me to not take things that weren't given to me. I knew she knew our plan and that made me angry. Albert was in Brussels for a wedding. We had wanted to take the amulet together, but I couldn't wait. Katarina thought she knew everything and I wanted to show her she didn't. I stole the amulet and rode all night to Brussels to the castle where Albert was staying.

"It was dawn as I rode up to the castle. There was a lone figure on the path. At first, I thought it was a castle guard. My horse spooked and unseated me. When I gained my bearings again, I realized it was Katarina. It was then I knew she was truly magic, for how did she, a mere woman, come to be at the castle before me? It was impossible."

"A mere woman?" I piped up. "Did you really just say that?"

He looked at me quizzically. "Mere woman? Yes, I did say it. It was the truth."

My face burned. No wonder Katarina had turned him into a frog. He was probably one of those princes who thought all women needed saving.

"She was calm," he continued, not noticing my anger. "She told me that because I had taken something that didn't belong to me, I must pay the price. I tried to give the amulet back but she said that it wasn't mine to give, that since I had stolen it, I must return it to the castle, which is where it was made long before she was born. Then she told me I would be cursed until my true love found me and broke the curse with a kiss. Once it was broken, if I didn't return the amulet to the throne room at

Geníru Castle in two midnight's time, my true love and I would both perish."

"Are you an absolute dunderhead?" I yelled. "You stole a witch's amulet after she warned you not to, got turned into a frog, and then got me into this mess too!"

"Your words do not make sense to me." Sebastián said, startled.

"She's saying that you…" Olive began, then shook her head. "Never mind, what she is saying. We need to get that amulet to Geníru."

"I no longer have it," Sebastián said, looking downcast. "It was in my pocket when I was cursed, but now it's gone."

"You lost it? We're both going to die. I don't want to die. I need to get back home. I need to see Nana and my parents. I—"

"Oh, calm down!" Olive snapped, stopping my panic. "I know where the amulet is."

Sebastián and I stared wide-eyed at Olive.

"Oh, come on Rosie, if you were only a little bit more interested in history, you would know too. It's in storage in a museum here in Brussels."

"How do you know this? You are just a girl," Sebastián said.

Olive rolled her eyes. "Girls know lots of things. We always have, plus I read an article about it. I've always been fascinated by Geníru. The Ruby Amulet is one of the only artifacts saved from Geníru. Mostly because it was found here in Brussels. Historians know quite a lot about Katarina.

She's actually mentioned more than you are. Most likely because historians could never figure out your name. It was like it was magically wiped from every record—which maybe it was, now that I know magic is real."

"Katarina is mentioned more than me?"

"Yes, dozens of books have been written about her."

"How can this be? I am the prince of Geníru. The people loved me."

Olive opened her mouth but I spoke first. "This is literally ancient history. How are we going to get this amulet?"

"We're going to have to steal it, of course." Olive smiled.

Chapter 6

"**O**live, are you out of your mind? We can't steal it. What about your four-year plan? Plus, that's how Sebastián got into this mess in the first place."

"It wouldn't technically be stealing. It doesn't belong to the museum. Besides, how else are we going to get it back to Geníru? We couldn't just waltz up to the museum curator and say, 'Oh, hello, we need that Ruby Amulet because my friend kissed a frog who turned out to be a prince and if we don't give the amulet back, she'll die.' And with you dead, half of my four-year plan is moot."

"That is a splendid idea." Sebastián smiled and stood up. "I simply will explain to this museum curator what has taken place. They will surely give me the amulet."

Olive pursed her lips and gave me The Look.

"Ah, let me help you, dear Rosie." Sebastián said as I began to stand up.

I nearly fell over as he lifted me off the ground and set me on my feet.

"In what direction does this museum curator live? We must make haste. We haven't a moment to spare," Sebastián said.

"I think it would be best to go with Olive's plan." I grabbed his arm. "The museum curator would think you were crazy or call the police—what you know as the guard."

"Surely they would give me the amulet. After all, I'm the prince of Geníru."

"You disappeared over three hundred years ago. No one lives for three hundred years. No one is going to believe you are the prince of Geníru."

"Yet you believe me."

"Because I kissed a frog and it turned into you. I can't unbelieve that."

"There must be witches who roam the earth today."

I shrugged. "Not any that I know of. Honestly, I didn't believe in witches until today. There was that one time when I was eight that I thought Nana was one, but that was only for a day."

He straightened his shoulders, his confidence returning. "Let us find this Nana."

"She's on the other side of the world and she's definitely not a witch." I groaned.

His shoulders slumped once more but then he straightened. "Well, then let's steal back the amulet!"

He began to move toward the busy street.

"Whoa!" I said, grabbing his arm. "You don't even know where this museum is and we need a plan. Madame Thomas is going to get suspicious. We can't just leave."

"Actually, we can. We have free time for the next few hours. Though we should probably get our room keys. And we need to find Sebastian some normal clothes. You're attracting way too much attention."

"What's wrong with my clothing?" Sebastián asked.

"It's three hundred years old." Olive snorted.

∞∞∞

Every part of me was wishing to be back in my hotel room at that moment and not in the museum. The building took my breath away but not because I was in awe of it. Oh, I should have been, but I'd been hoping that I would wake up from this crazy dream before we reached the museum. No such luck. This fairytale was reality.

My hands shook as Olive brought the Ruby Amulet toward me.

"This will work perfectly," she said brightly as the gift shop door swung closed behind her.

Through the gift shop window, I could see at least a dozen Ruby Amulets still hanging from a hook.

"Should we buy another fake one just in

case?" I asked.

"No, we only need one," Olive replied.

"I cannot believe that this isn't the real amulet," Sebastián said, studying it closely. "How did they make a replica that is this precise?"

"It's made out of plastic." Olive replied, not really answering the question. "Here, keep this in your pocket."

He took it and put it in his new jacket pocket. Honestly, the new clothes didn't make him stand out any less. The one thing people of three hundred years ago had on us was how physically fit they had to be. Long hours in a desk at school and office jobs had not done our bodies any favors. It made me want to make a new year's resolution to train like a medieval soldier—maybe then I could open the jam jar by myself.

"You all remember the plan?" Olive asked, pulling me out of my wandering thoughts.

Sebastián and I both nodded. Olive smiled once more and took the lead. She strode confidently toward the front desk.

"If she wasn't a woman I would put in her charge of an army. Her brain is keen on strategy," Sebastián whispered to me.

I snorted. He could be so annoying sometimes, but could I really judge him by today's standards? It didn't seem fair. A lot had changed in three hundred years.

Thirty minutes later, we stood in the main curator's office with Olive pleading her point.

"I'm such a fan of Katarina's and I would really love to see her amulet. I know it's in storage but is there any way we could see it? I wouldn't touch it or anything."

The curator tapped her chin. "If you're a real fan then you would be able to tell me how Katarina healed all the cattle in the kingdom of Geníru when they mysteriously fell ill."

Olive sucked in her breath and that's when I knew she didn't know. We were doomed if this was a test.

"She sang to them and they began to dance," Sebastián said. "It was quite a lovely song."

I stepped on his foot.

"Or at least that is what the legends say," he added.

The curator looked astonished. "You really are fans. That is one of the lesser known tales. Come along. Just promise not to touch anything. I'm only an intern. The actual curator has the day off."

Olive gave Sebastián a high five and he looked thoroughly confused by it. We followed the intern through a labyrinth of hallways. We passed by several doors until she stopped in front of one.

"This is where we keep everything from the old Geníru exhibit. I hope to put it on display again in the future but people seem to have lost interest in the country. It's good to know there are still some young people who are future historians."

"To be a historian is one of my life goals," Olive said, and she wasn't lying.

She'd had a history-themed party for her fifth birthday. She kept saying, 'let them eat cake' and waltzing around like she was a queen one moment and then the next she'd scream something about a guillotine. She'd made us answer historical trivia about cake before she'd give us a slice. Luckily, her parents had intervened and made sure we all got some.

The intern opened the door to a room full of boxes. She took a small box down from a shelf and carefully opened it. Inside lay the Ruby Amulet. It seemed to pulse with magic. We all stared at it for a moment and then Olive spoke up

"I don't feel so good. I think I'm going to faint." She began teetering dramatically and I was sure the intern wouldn't be fooled.

The intern's eyes grew large. "Oh, my goodness, sit down."

The intern helped Olive to sit on the floor. Olive covered her face with her hands.

"I think I might puke." She groaned.

I was so captivated by Olive's performances I nearly forgot to grab the Ruby Amulet from the box. Sebastián nudged my arm, bringing me back to the present. I looked at the intern. She was still fussing around Olive. I reached into the box and clasped my hand around the amulet. It was surprisingly warm. It was large, about the size of the palm of my hand. I held it behind my back away from the intern's view.

Sebastián placed the fake amulet in the box. It didn't look quite right. If the intern looked at it, she would definitely be able to tell it wasn't the real Ruby Amulet.

"I'm going to go get Mr. Vinny. He used to be a doctor," the intern announced. "Stay right here and don't touch anything."

We watched as she rushed from the room.

"This isn't going to work," I whispered. "It looks nothing like the real one."

"It's the best we've got. Hopefully she won't look at it before she closes the box," Olive told me from her seat on the floor.

"Someone will look eventually and then they'll realize we took it."

I held up the real Ruby Amulet next to the fake one. The real one seemed to shine while the fake was just dull.

"I wish they looked the same," I said.

The amulet in my hand grew hot but it didn't burn me. It began to glow and it shot out a small strand of light toward the fake medallion. I blinked. The fake medallion began to look more and more like the real one. When the glow faded, I couldn't spot a difference between the two.

Olive had stood up as soon as the amulet began to glow and her mouth was gaping open.

"It really is magic," I said in awe.

Sebastián took a step back. "'Tis indeed. I'll not have any more to do with it. I don't want another curse upon me."

"I'll carry it," I said as I put it around my neck and hid it under my jacket.

"What are you doing?" Olive asked.

"I don't want to lose it," I shot back. "My pockets aren't big enough."

Olive opened her mouth to respond, but we heard voices coming down the hallway. She resumed her spot on the floor and tried to look ill once more.

And just like that, we'd stolen a priceless artifact from a museum.

Chapter 7

After Olive made a miraculous recovery, the intern called us a cab to take us back to the hotel. Olive had persuaded the cab driver to drop us off at a store instead. She walked purposefully down the aisles as I tried to keep my hand from going to the Ruby Amulet hiding under my jacket. More heat radiated from it each step I took.

Olive plucked a map off the stand and paid the clerk. Sebastian and I followed her out of the store. He'd been oddly quiet since we left the museum.

"Are you okay?" I asked tentatively.

He shrugged. "It was odd to see one's things packed away in a box and become an old relic. That woman said no one really cared about Geníru anymore. It's as if it never existed. My country had been a country far longer than France. At least, it had been three hundred years ago, and now it is gone."

I bit my lip. How would it be to suddenly

have your whole life ripped away from you with nothing familiar left? Sure, my life had been turned upside down last year when my parents broke contact with Nana and Papa. I'd always thought it was odd that my mom had disowned her parents. But I still knew Nana and Papa were out there, well and alive. I still had many things that were the same from a year ago. Olive was still the same Olive, I still practiced French, I still had my parents and my little brother. Everything Sebastián had ever known was simply gone. It must be terrifying.

I grabbed his hand and squeezed it. "I'm sorry. You paid an awful price."

He smiled. "I was warned and it was a price I had to pay."

"What do you suppose happened to your cousin Albert? Did he pay a price for putting the idea into your head?"

"He was next in line for the throne. Unless something horrible happened, he most likely became King."

"He did," Olive piped up.

Sebastián grimaced "How was he as King?"

"Quite mad, as you would say," Olive said, picking her words carefully. "He married your betrothed."

"He married Isabella?" he replied in shock.

"You were betrothed?" I squeaked, taking my hand from his.

"Yes, everyone of my station was betrothed. Is it not the same today?"

"No," Olive and I responded together.

"Then how do countries form strong alliances?" Then he sighed. "Never mind, what happened with Albert?"

"He and Isabella had six children. One boy and five girls."

"What rotten luck," Sebastián exclaimed. "All those children, but just one boy."

I was beginning to regret feeling bad for him.

"Unfortunately, their son Charles was quite mad as well. Much more so than his father. He drove the kingdom to ruin. His sister Margaret had been married off to a French royal and he claimed Geníru for France. There wasn't much resistance at that point."

"Albert married his daughter off to France? That is against our law in Geníru!"

"Is it really? I didn't know that bit," Olive replied. "If it makes you feel any better, the French Revolution happened soon after and that particular royal lost his head. Margaret escaped to England with their children."

"What revolution?"

"The French Revolution, where the people deposed the king of France," I told him.

"Who is the king now?" he asked.

"No one is. They don't have a king anymore."

"What madness is this? No king? How does their country survive?"

"I'm beginning to think it's a good thing you turned into a frog when you did," I replied, ignoring his questions. "I don't think you would have liked the second half of the eighteenth century."

"We don't exactly have time for this now." Olive opened the map. "It's getting late and we need a plan. We also need to figure out where the Geníru Castle is."

"I know where my castle is," Sebastián huffed.

"You knew three hundred years ago. A lot has changed and now historians can't even agree where the castle of Geníru was."

She stared down at the map. "Geníru was right here."

"Bah. No it isn't," Sebastián retorted. "It's right here. Do you see the two rivers? That is the best landmark for finding Geníru."

He was pointing a little to the north of where Olive had pointed.

"Where is the castle then?" I asked.

"It used to lie in the middle of the valley." He tapped his chin.

Olive tilted her head. "None of the historians believe it was there. They all say it was further south."

"And none of them have found it, have they?" Sebastián asked.

"No."

"Because they were looking in the wrong place." He smiled broadly, as if he was the smartest person alive.

"He does have a point, Olive," I stated. "Plus,

he did grow up in Geníru. I know things have changed, but it's our best bet."

She nodded. "You're right. I guess we better start looking at bus or train routes and plan our escape. Our parents might kill us for this."

"Probably."

"I will defend both of you. I cannot let my one true love die, or her dear friend." Sebastián puffed out his chest.

I shook my head. He could be a bit too much at times. I was beginning to think the magic had been wrong. No way could he be my one true love. Besides, Mom always said there was no such thing as a soulmate or one true love.

"Alright, how are we going to sneak out tonight without Madame Thomas noticing?" I asked, trying to ignore my whirling thoughts.

"You're sneaking out? I want in."

"Don't forget about me in this plan."

We whirled around to see Jeremey and Nathan both smiling goofily at us.

"So, what are we sneaking out for? A midnight pizza run? A movie? Wait, are we going to a club?" Jeremey asked.

I glanced at Olive. She seemed to be thinking the same thing as me—now what?

Chapter 8

"**W**e're going to find the long-lost castle of Geníru," Olive said in a matter-of-fact tone.

"Olive!" Sebastián and I cried at the same time.

"What? There's no use in lying to them." Olive gave us a wink. "This is our friend Sebastián. His dad's an archeologist trying to find the castle, but we think he's looking in the wrong place."

"Why don't you just tell your dad that instead of trying to find it yourself?" Nathan asked Sebastián.

"He…How do you Americans say…he doesn't listen," Sebastián responded, surprising me with his acting skills.

"Typical parents," Jeremey said, glaring at him a little. "Well, I'm in."

"You can't come with us," I snapped.

"Yes I can, or I can go tell Madame Thomas what you're all up to."

I was about ready to bite his head off when Sebastián said, "We could use the help of strong capable men."

Olive rolled her eyes. "How medieval of you."

"I'm a bit lost," Nathan said. "Is anyone else?"

"It looks like you're both coming with us," I told him and Jeremey. "We may need your help fighting off a dragon or something."

Nathan and Jeremey both laughed.

"Why are they laughing?" Sebastián whispered to me. "Dragons are cunning and wise. Certainly not a laughing matter."

My eyes widened. Dragons were real? Or they had at least been real a few hundred years ago.

"They're renowned dragon hunters," I lied.

Sebastián looked at the boys then back at me. "Are you sure?"

I nodded. "Yep, some of the best."

Sebastián straightened and then shook both of their hands. "It is a pleasure to meet both of you..."

"Jeremey and Nathan," I supplied.

Sebastián nodded and released Jeremey's hand. Jeremey stretched his hand out as if the handshake had hurt. He didn't look pleased to meet Sebastián.

"It's getting late. Let's all meet back here at ten tonight," Olive said. "Don't get caught sneaking out, and if you do, tell Madame Thomas you were sneaking out for pizza."

"I will await your return, dear Rosie," Sebastián said, placing a kiss on my hand.

My face grew warm. I could feel the others' eyes on me.

"See you later," I told him, prying my hand from his.

"The guy really is medieval. Do you think he's an actor?" Nathan murmured to Jeremey on the way back to the hotel.

∞ ∞ ∞

Somehow, sneaking out had gone without a hitch. Jeremey and Nathan met us outside the hotel and we hurried to find Sebastián. He was right where we'd left him. He was staring up into the night sky thoughtfully.

"Have the stars died?" he asked. "I cannot see them."

"Oh, they're still up there. It's just hard to see them because of light pollution," I said, grabbing his hand and pulling him to his feet.

"Light pollution?" he asked.

"It doesn't matter at the moment," Olive told him. "We've got a bus to catch."

"Has everyone turned off their phones?" Jeremey asked as we ran.

"Oh, right," Olive exclaimed, taking out her phone. "We don't want to be tracked."

I didn't have a phone. My parents had told me I wasn't old enough for one yet. Even though most of my friends had them by the time we were twelve.

"That little device tracks you?" Sebastián whispered, looking concerned and confused.

"It can, and it can call and message people on the other side of the world," I replied, out of breath as we continued to run.

We made it to the bus stop with no time to spare and Olive paid for tickets. Nathan was sweetly trying to explain what light pollution was to Sebastián as Jeremey glared daggers at him. Sebastián didn't seem to notice Jeremey's glare. We all piled onto the bus and found seats near each other.

Olive pulled out her map, drawing Nathan's attention.

"The bus ride will be about four hours," she said, squinting at the map in the dim light.

Nathan pointed to the red x mark on the map that Olive must have added. "This is where you believe the castle to be?"

"Yes," Olive replied.

"Aren't the woods there supposed to be haunted?" he asked.

"You've heard those stories too?" Olive replied with wide eyes.

"I read a book about folktales regarding this area before the trip." He smiled. He looked at Olive for half a second but then looked away.

"Haunted?" Jeremey asked, looking concerned.

Olive shrugged. "A lot of weird things have happened in the area."

"And we are going there?" he asked.

"I'm sure it's just stuff of fairytales," I told them, trying to calm my own rapidly beating heart. "If it's going to be four hours maybe we should all get some sleep."

"That sounds like a good plan," Olive said, folding up the map and putting it in her backpack.

I leaned against the window and tried not to think about the haunted woods. It sounded like stuff of fairytales. If I'd been told this yesterday I would have laughed it off, but today was different. Today I'd learned fairytales were real.

∞∞∞

I woke up as my head bumped the seat in front of me. The bus came to a screeching halt.

"What's going on?" I asked as I rubbed my head.

My friends all wore the same dazed expression that I wore and Sebastián seemed to be on high alert. His hand reached for a sword that wasn't there.

The bus driver was saying something in French. My tired brain only had a second to translate it.

"One of the tires blew," I told everyone.

"We know, Rosie. We all speak French." Olive said as she grabbed her backpack.

We joined the crowd around the bus driver.

"How long until it's fixed?" One passenger called in French.

"Perhaps three hours," the driver responded.

Oh fiddlesticks! I looked at my watch. It was one in the morning. I had less than twenty-four hours to get the Ruby Amulet back to Geníru castle. As if it knew I was thinking of it, the amulet became warm again.

"How many miles left?" I asked Olive.

"Based on the time, I'd say we still have about ten miles."

"We should walk."

"Ten miles is pretty far," Olive replied.

"We could walk ten miles in less than three hours," I persisted.

"Why the rush?" Jeremey asked.

"The longer we're gone, the sooner someone will notice," I told him. "I don't want to get caught until we find the castle."

"All right then," Sebastián said. "We walk."

Chapter 9

It was cold, but it felt good to be moving. I didn't want to stop walking. Moving got me closer to finding the castle and farther away from a cursed death.

"Look, the stars are back!" Sebastián said in awe from beside me.

I looked up into the night sky. Thousands upon thousands of stars glowed, casting their light upon us. Olive, Jeremey, and Nathan were in front of us. Olive was telling them about some historical fact about the road we were on. Who knew roads could have a history?

"Rosie, may I ask you a question?" Sebastián spoke up.

"Sure."

"What is an archeologist?"

"Someone who digs in the dirt for old cities." I shrugged. I wasn't quite sure what it was but in movies that's what they seemed to do.

"Do you suppose Geníru Castle is buried under the ground?"

"I hope not. I don't think it will be. It's only been three hundred years. Usually archeologists dig for ancient cities that are thousands of years old."

"Why would anyone do that? Dig for cities that are buried?"

"I guess to learn more about where we come from. How people lived a thousand years ago."

"Where do you come from?" Sebastián asked. "Do you have a family with brothers and sisters?"

His questions took me by surprise but I decided to answer them. We were, after all, supposed to be each other's one true love and maybe if I got to know him better, I would like him better.

"I have a younger brother. He's ten but I think he's smart for a ten-year-old. He would be able to tell you all about light pollution and cell phones. My parents are lawyers and they can be boring, but they make sure to make time for us kids. Then there is my Nana and Papa, my…"

I trailed off. Perhaps I didn't want to tell him about Nana and Papa not yet.

"Who are Nana and Papa?" he asked, prompting me to continue.

"They are my mother's parents. My parents had me when they were young. They weren't done with school yet so I spent a lot of time with Nana and Papa growing up. They're from Belgium. Nana taught me everything I know about French. Papa is really good with animals. I used to think he could talk to them. They're two of my most favorite people."

"I think I would like to meet this Nana and Papa."

"I would like to see them as well." I sighed.

"You miss them?"

"I haven't seen them in a year."

"That doesn't seem so long," Sebastián said.

"Maybe for your time period but for mine it is. I haven't even been able to call them on the phone —that magical device that lets you talk to anyone even if they are on the other side of the world."

"Why not?"

I shrugged as tears came to my eyes. "My parents had an argument with them. I don't even know what it was about. My parents won't tell me. They just say it's stuff I wouldn't understand. I want to know why. None of it makes any sense. If I knew why then maybe I would understand why I can't speak to or see them. I keep feeling like there's a horrible battle going on inside me. The part that is loyal to and loves my parents and the part that loves my grandparents. How is it fair for my parents to not tell me why I can't speak to them?"

I turned my face away from Sebastián, embarrassed as angry tears trailed down my cheeks. This was a bad idea. I shouldn't have even started to tell him about my family, let alone Nana and Papa. Sebastián grabbed my hand and squeezed it. Warmth flew up my arm.

I turned back toward him.

"I'm sorry, dear Rosie. It is hard when people you love don't love each other."

I nodded.

"My parents were like that. They had an arranged marriage. My mother was a disappointment to my father as she only ever had one child—me. I often felt in the middle of the games they played to hurt each other."

"That's awful!"

He shrugged. "It's all part of the past now. How angry my father must have been after I disappeared! He would have hated to give his throne to Albert."

I looked at him, wishing I could see his eyes so I could know what he was thinking. Maybe I was lucky to have the family I did have. We continued to hold hands as we walked down the road. Sebastián seemed to be deep in thought and not paying attention to where he was going. As we neared a mud puddle, I steered him out of the way.

He looked shocked. "I didn't even see that puddle."

"I just saved your life." I laughed.

He smiled. "When we get to my castle in Geníru I will have to find one of our medals for bravery and give it to you for saving me from soggy shoes."

Our laughter was stopped short by Jeremey. "Your castle? Just who do you think you are?"

Sebastián puffed out his chest. "I'm Prince Sebastián III of Geníru."

"That isn't possible. Geníru hasn't been a country for three hundred years," Nathan piped up.

"Well, that's true," I began. "But I kissed a frog and it turned into a prince."

Jeremey's eyes widened. "Are you both crazy?"

I glared at him. "Don't call me crazy!"

"She's telling the truth, Jeremey," Olive said, coming to my defense.

"You believe all this?"

"Yes, I do," Olive shot back.

"Prove it."

Anger flared through me and I pulled the amulet out from underneath my jacket. "This is an amulet from the witch who cursed Sebastián. It's all the proof I have."

"Where did you get that from?" Nathan asked with trepidation.

"A museum in Brussels."

"We're all going to be in so much trouble," he muttered.

"Give me that," Jeremey said, reaching for the amulet.

I tried to pull it away but he was quicker than I. He grabbed it and it instantly began to glow red. It grew in brightness until I wanted to close my eyes. Jeremey tried to pull his hand away from the Ruby Amulet but he couldn't. Just when I thought I couldn't stand the brightness any longer, it faded. Jeremey yelped as if the amulet had bit him and it fell from his hand.

"It burned me," he cried.

"That's because it's magic and we have to re-turn it by midnight, otherwise me and Sebastián die."

"But why did it burn me?"

I calmed down. "Because you asked for proof."

And though I didn't know how I'd known that, I knew it was true.

Chapter 10

J eremey paced back and forth on the muddy road, muttering under his breath. I caught snatches of what he said.

"Magic...not real...burned my finger...he's a prince! How am I supposed to compete with a prince?"

My face burned and I took a step back from him, hoping to avoid hearing anything else. I grabbed the amulet. It was still warm but it didn't burn me. I caught Sebastian's eye. He was looking at the amulet with a mix of terror and awe.

"Where did the Ruby Amulet come from?" I asked him.

He shook his head. "I always believed it to be Katarina's. I didn't know it had been given to her."

"Legends say that the ruby was mined from the ground where the castle was built. It was the heart of the castle. The heart of Geníru. Throughout generations, it was passed down to wise woman to guard and protect," Olive spoke up.

"How do you know this?" Sebastián asked.

She shrugged. "I like reading and I was obsessed with Geníru when I was younger. It seemed like a place where fairytales were possible. That's part of the reason I wanted to come on this trip. I knew we would be close to where historians believed Geníru to be."

"You're quite brilliant," Sebastián said.

I noticed he didn't add *for a girl*. Perhaps I was rubbing off on him.

Olive beamed. "Thank you!"

I looked back at Jeremey. Nathan had put his hand on Jeremey's shoulder, stopping his pacing. They were talking in hushed tones. Jeremey nodded at something Nathan said and they came to join us. I stiffened. What if Jeremey and Nathan decided to leave? Would they tell Madame Thomas where we were before we had the chance to make it to Geníru?

"Well?" Olive asked, looking at them expectantly.

"We're still coming with you," Nathan told her.

Her face lit up in another smile.

"As long as Rosie keeps that thing away from me," Jeremey said, pointing a shaky finger at the amulet.

I nodded in agreement. The Ruby Amulet had rattled us all. Angry red blisters were forming on Jeremey's fingers where he'd touched it.

"Onward on our quest!" Sebastián proclaimed, making the rest of us laugh.

He looked around, questioning. "I said nothing that should make one laugh."

I shook my head. "People don't really say things like that anymore."

"Well, they should. We are on a quest."

"If we're on a quest shouldn't it have a name like the quest for the Holy Grail?" Jeremey asked, returning to his goofy self.

"Yeah, but we aren't searching for the Holy Grail," Nathan added.

"We could call ourselves the Avengers of Geníru," Olive said.

"We aren't really avenging anything," Jeremey replied. "And there are way too many avengers these days."

"I've been on many quests and we have never named it," Sebastián responded.

"Well, man, you've been doing this whole questing business wrong then." Jeremey yawned.

"Every good quest has got to have a name." Nathan laughed.

"Why don't we just call it The Quest of the Ruby Amulet? Short and simple," I interjected.

"That's the perfect name," Olive said.

"Not too fancy," Jeremey agreed, and Nathan nodded in approval.

We turned to Sebastián. He looked pensive standing in the moonlight. He stared at us as if he was trying to figure out where the last few pieces of a complex puzzle went, then he grinned.

"The Quest of the Ruby Amulet is a fine name and a worthy quest for any knights of Geníru."

"Are we knights now?" Nathan asked.

Sebastián nodded. "Indeed. I, as the last true ruler of Geníru, knight you, Jeremey, and you, Nathan."

Nathan smiled and Jeremey crowed into the night air.

"Can I be a knight as well?" Olive asked.

Sebastián paused before a smile lit up his face. "Lady Olive, I knight you the first lady knight of Geníru. A wiser knight cannot be found in all the land."

Olive giggled and gave a small curtsy.

I smiled at Sebastián. "And what about me, my prince? Shall you knight me as well?"

Sebastián looked grave as he shook his head. "I fear not, for you are the fair maiden that we are rescuing and our quest is dedicated to you."

Sebastián kneeled on the road, bowing to me. Olive, Jeremey, and Nathan clumsily followed suit. I wanted to roll my eyes but for some reason I found it endearing.

"Rise, my prince and loyal knights," I said, trying to sound regal as I held back a laugh.

They rose and, in the process, Sebastián took my hand and kissed it. The warmth of the kiss took my breath away and made my heart flutter.

"Let us press onward and rescue the fair Lady Rosie," Sebastián cried.

Olive, Nathan, and Jeremey gave a cheer and

began walking down the road again. Olive slung one arm around Jeremey and the other around Nathan. Sebastián took my hand and we followed them. I looked up at the night sky. The stars seemed numberless as they glittered like tiny jewels in the darkness. I smiled. At this moment, with perhaps millions of stars shining down on me, I felt truly happy —even if the circumstances were less than ideal. I had less than twenty-four hours to break the last part of the curse and if I didn't, I would die. But here on this country road, surrounded by friends, my heart was joyful.

I turned my head to look at Sebastián. "You know, you got one thing wrong."

"What is that?"

I cocked an eyebrow. "I'm going to be the one rescuing you."

Chapter 11

Olive hissed with pain as she walked. She was limping ever so slightly. Jeremey seemed to be walking as if in a dream as he stumbled down the road. Nathan and Sebastián were walking as if they still had all the energy in the world. It was all I could do to keep one foot in front of the other. Olive took another hissing step and fell onto the damp road.

Nathan immediately jumped into action, helping her up from the ground. "Are you alright?"

She smiled weakly. "I'm fine."

"Your shoe is split open," Nathan said, pointing at Olive's foot.

"Olive!" I cried. "Why didn't you tell us?"

"I didn't want to slow anyone down. Does anyone have duct tape? Maybe I could just tape it back together. I should have listened to my parents when they said I should get new shoes for this trip."

"How many miles do you think we've

walked? Are we close?" Jeremey yawned.

"Five miles," Sebastián and Nathan said at the same time.

They gave each other an appraising look.

"Are you sure?" I asked.

They both nodded.

"How can you tell?" Jeremey asked.

Sebastián shrugged. "I remember the map Olive showed me."

"I have a mile counter on my watch," Nathan said sheepishly.

"At this rate we won't make it for another two hours." I sighed. "It was a bad idea to leave the bus."

Olive's eyes brightened. "We still have our bus tickets! There is another stop on this road. Maybe we could wait there for the bus?"

We all murmured in agreement. At the rate we were going, one of us was bound to drop before we made the rest of the journey.

"You can't walk with your shoe like that," Nathan told Olive. "I'll give you a piggyback ride."

"Are you sure you can carry me?" Olive asked.

"Yep," he said, puffing out his chest.

I rolled my eyes but then stopped myself. Who was I to think it silly that Nathan wanted to impress Olive? Nathan was kind and smart and a lot better than most boys I knew.

"Allow me to carry your bag, Lady Olive," Sebastián volunteered.

"Thank you," she said as she handed him her

backpack.

Nathan knelt down and Olive hopped onto his back. To his credit, he didn't even grunt when he stood up and started walking. I was beginning to wonder if Nathan was an avid backpacker.

"Are you alright, my love?" Sebastián asked me as we continued to walk down the road.

"Yes, only tired and I feel a bit foolish for insisting we get off the bus," I told him. "Why do you keep calling me your love?"

"You broke the curse," he replied simply. "Only true love's kiss could break the curse."

"But I don't even know you. Love usually takes time. Lots of time."

"Perhaps Katarina knew we would eventually fall in love and it would be true love."

"Perhaps" was all I responded with.

Magic was pretty convincing when it came to helping a person find their true love, but it also seemed too sudden. I was just fifteen. I had my whole life to live and find true love. What if I was actually missing out on my real true love because of Sebastián?

I shook my head. I was thinking about it too much. Mom had always said there wasn't such a thing as one true love. So maybe Sebastián and I really could have that one in a million type of love, but it didn't mean we had to, did it?

"I see the sign for the bus stop." Jeremey jumped with glee, showing more energy than he had for the past hour, providing my brain a much-needed distraction.

Jeremey raced toward the sign and Nathan skipped the rest of the way, causing Olive to laugh as she bounced around. There was one lone bench at the stop that we all squished onto.

"How's your foot?" I asked Olive as we huddled next to each other.

"I'll be fine. I'll just need to find new shoes before we go into the forest." She laid her head on my shoulder.

I was beginning to feel like a bad friend. Olive was so brave and smart. She hadn't complained once about her foot even though it must be throbbing with pain.

She gave my hand a squeeze. "Don't worry. It will all work out."

I got a warm fuzzy feeling in my heart. I was lucky to have such an amazing friend. Even though I didn't know if I would still be alive tomorrow, Olive had faith that everything would be okay and I could trust her on that.

$$\infty \; \infty \; \infty$$

A bus horn blared and Jeremey yelped as he fell off the edge of the bench. I opened my eyes. It was bright and sunny once more and a bus was stopping in front of us. We all groggily got up and filed onto the bus. It was the same bus driver from the night before.

The driver gave us a funny look and said, "Decided you couldn't outwalk the bus, eh?"

I nodded as we found empty seats by each other.

"What did the driver say?" Olive yawned. "My brain is too tired to translate French to English."

I laughed. "I didn't even realize he spoke in French. He said, 'decided you couldn't outwalk the bus, eh?'"

"Is eh even a French word?" Nathan asked.

"No, but he said something like that."

We all started laughing but I stopped when I noticed a fellow passenger looking at us strangely. When he noticed me staring, he went back to looking at his phone. I caught him looking at us several more times and I got the uncomfortable feeling that he knew who we were.

I looked at my watch and bit back a groan. It was eight-thirty in the morning. The bus must have been delayed more than we thought it would be. I took a deep breath, trying to stave off the panic. I would be fine. I had a prince and three brave and loyal knights. Wait a second, I had myself too. I was a strong, independent female. I could do anything, but a little help wouldn't hurt.

It was hardly any time before the bus pulled into a charming little village and came to a stop in a shopping area.

"It's so pretty here," Olive sighed as we stood to walk off the bus.

I nodded in agreement. "Let's find you some new shoes."

It seemed the stores were just opening as we walked in. Jeremey and Nathan went off to find some chocolate and they convinced Sebastián to go along.

"What is this chocolate?" I heard him ask as they walked away.

Olive and I decided to ask the cashier where the shoes were. The cashier was busy putting boxes away so we waited. A tv was on, broadcasting the morning news, and I caught snatches of what it said.

I glanced over at the tv and stared in horror. Olive grabbed my arm. She'd noticed as well. On the screen were pictures of Jeremey, Nathan, Olive, and I.

Chapter 12

The cashier was beginning to turn around. She was going to see us. Would she recognize us? Olive was more quick thinking than I was and she grabbed my arm, forcing me to turn around and walk away.

We darted in between aisles, trying to avoid any other customers. We finally caught sight of the boys and rushed to them.

"We have a big problem," I began.

"They know we're missing. Our pictures are on the tv. We need to lay low. Perhaps just get into the forest now," Olive finished.

"Calm down," Nathan replied, raising his hands in the air. "They don't know where we're at."

"I think they do," I said, biting my lip. "That guy on the bus kept staring at us like he knew us. If we get caught, we'll never make it to Geníru Castle."

"I do not understand most of the words you are saying, but may I assume that my picture is not on this tv?" Sebastián interrupted.

"No." I sighed in relief.

"Then may I suggest that we find a place for you to all lay low, as you put it, and I will scout the area."

"I still need shoes or duct tape," Olive insisted.

"Sebastián can find some for you," I told her. "Right now, we can't let anyone see us."

"It might be too late for that," Nathan said, his eyes widening.

We followed his gaze and saw two police officers. They were questioning the cashier, effectively blocking our exit. My heart sank. We were doomed!

Sebastián put his hand on my shoulder. "Don't lose faith, dear Rosie."

He turned to the others. "Alas, knights, we are tasked with our first real battle. What is our plan of attack?"

Jeremey cracked a smile.

"There must be another exit" Olive stated, looking around. Then she pointed with her chin. "There, in the back of the store."

"It doesn't say exit. What if it's just a storeroom?" Nathan put in.

"We don't have a better option at the moment," Jeremey said. "Everyone get down, they're coming this way."

We all ducked low enough that the store shelves hid us from view.

"This way," Jeremey directed as we hurried

through the aisle.

We rounded a corner and froze. A woman holding a baby on her hip stared at us questioningly.

"We dropped some money," I said in a perfect French accent. "We're just looking for it."

The confusion on her face lessened but her suspicion didn't. Instead of replying, she shook her head and muttered something that sounded like 'teenagers' under her breath before walking away.

Jeremey waved us forward again and we continued our escape. We'd crossed three aisles when he came to a halt and we nearly plowed into him.

"Back up, back up, back up," he urged.

I snuck a peek around the corner. The police officers were walking down the aisle. The woman holding her baby was stopped by them. She pointed to where we had come from and they turned.

"Now," Jeremey hissed, and we rushed the unmarked door. The room was filled with shelves and boxes. I didn't see an exit in sight.

Jeremey took the lead once more, scouring the room for some sort of escape. We all froze as we heard voices on the other side of the door we had come through.

"I found it!" Jeremey whispered. "Well, I found something. It's a door they use for delivery."

He pulled on a chain and the delivery door opened with a load groan.

We rushed through it. Jeremey let go of the chain and dived under the door as it crashed back down.

"That made me feel like Indiana Jones." He laughed.

"Come on," Nathan said, pulling him up.

And then we ran. We took back alleyways and streets, avoiding people. Olive paused in our flight to kick off her shoes. She scooped them up and hurried to catch up to us. Sebastián skittered to a halt in front of a door of a building that looked abandoned. He rammed his shoulder into the door before any of us could protest. It opened to what looked to be an old forgotten dance hall.

We all collapsed on the dusty floor inside as he shut the door behind us.

"That was awesome," Jeremey huffed.

I bit back a laugh. It had been exhilarating but it had also been too close.

"Now what?" Olive asked, pulling out her map. "I didn't even keep track of the way we ran. We could have gone in the wrong direction."

"I will go find out," Sebastián said, climbing to his feet.

"But you could get caught," I protested, fear rising in me.

"My picture was not on the magic tv. No one has seen my portrait," he stated. "I will scout the area. That was the plan and I will find Lady Olive new shoes."

"But that woman in the store saw you with us."

"She did not see my face," Sebastián reassured me. "And now I know what the knights of this time look like. Do they all dress like that?”

"I think so. I'm not really sure.”

"I shall be careful.” He placed a kiss on my hand and then he was gone.

Olive sighed dramatically. "He's not coming back with the correct shoe size, is he?”

I snorted. "Probably not.”

Chapter 13

I looked at my watch once more. It was eleven. Sebastián had been gone for nearly two hours. That was two hours less time we had to find Geníru. Had he been caught? Had he gotten lost? Did he go to find the castle on his own?

I looked around the old dance hall. It must have been magnificent at one time. Cobwebs were wrapped intricately around a massive chandelier, and even though the floors were dusty I could see they were wood.

Jeremey was sprawled out, sleeping in one corner of room, while Nathan tossed a small ball he had found back and forth between his hands. I glanced over at Olive. She was hefting open another crate. There had been several stacked in the corner. The first one had contained stacks of old letters. I looked over her shoulder into the crate. This one was filled with intricate glass party decorations.

"It's a bit sad, isn't it?" she asked as she pulled

out a replica of a glass slipper. "These once probably meant a great deal to someone and now they're stuffed in a box long forgotten about. I wonder if that's how all our lives will be. In two hundred years, everything I owned will most likely be in a dusty old box and no one will remember my name."

"Aren't you being a bit too philosophical?" I said in return as I pulled out a miniature blown glass carriage.

She shrugged. "Sebastián was born over three hundred years ago and no one remembers his name and he was royalty. Doesn't that seem odd to you?"

"Maybe it was because of the curse. Perhaps no one could remember his name?"

She tapped a finger to her lips. "There are lots of fairytales where people are cursed and they still have names. Like Snow White."

"I doubt that was her real name…at least, I hope it wasn't her real name."

Olive smiled a little. "I just think it's odd, that's all. Three hundred years isn't that long ago."

"Do you think Katarina erased his name from history to be cruel?" I asked as I marveled at a glass flower.

Olive shook her head. "In all the stories I've read about her, she doesn't seem like a cruel person. Even Sebastián doesn't think so. She just seemed wise. It would have been great to talk to her. Maybe she could have seen my future."

I shivered. "Do you think she could still be alive?"

"No, her death was recorded in history. She died of old age. She knew the day she would die—or at least, that's what legend says." Olive turned toward me, her eyes alight with excitement. "Rosie, I completely forgot! How could I have forgotten?"

"What are you talking about? What did you forget?"

"The day Katarina died, it's said she told her friends and loved ones goodbye and gave one final prophecy. The Ruby Amulet would be returned by a forgotten prince and a girl with golden curls who would save Geníru."

The hair on my arms stood straight up and I shivered. "You're teasing me, Olive."

She shook her head, her eyes still bright. "No, I'm not. I'd just forgotten."

"It can't be true still. I may have golden curls, but I can't save Geníru. It doesn't exist anymore."

Olive furrowed her brow. "Well, that is what Katarina said and she would know, as she placed the curse on Sebastián."

It was my turn to shake my head, only this time in disbelief. "What happened after she spoke that prophecy?"

Olive's face fell a little. "She lay on her bed, closed her eyes, and died. The legends always used the term 'slipped away' instead of died. It's said that even the birds and flowers mourned her death."

The mood in the room felt instantly melancholy and I touched the Ruby Amulet. Its warmth spread through my fingers.

"Do you think it was the Ruby Amulet that made her live for so long?" I asked.

"It must have been," Olive said, putting the glass trinkets carefully back into the crate and closing the lid. "She died soon after it was lost. I never really believed she was as old as the legends said. At least, not until I met Sebastián."

The main door burst open and I nearly screamed. I let out a breath I hadn't even known I been holding when I realized it was only Sebastián.

"My apologies for startling all of you," he said, tipping his head. "I was having trouble opening the door."

We were all standing now and I noticed Nathan was holding the ball, ready to throw it at Sebastián.

"May I have some help?" he asked.

Nathan rushed forward to take some of the things from Sebastian's arms. Jeremey closed the door carefully behind him.

"Is that a hunk of cheese?" I asked.

"*Oui*, I thought you all might be famished," Sebastián replied with a dazzling smile.

As if on cue, my stomach growled. I hadn't eaten anything since dinner the night before.

"I also brought some bread and fruit. 'Tis marvelous that this day and age has fresh fruit. In my time, it was hard to find during certain seasons. Now it seems that everyone lives as a king, even the peasants."

"Peasants don't really exist anymore," I told

him, grabbing the offered roll.

Sebastián placed a pair of boots in Olive's hands. "Fine footwear for you, Lady Olive."

"You got the right size," Olive said in amazement.

"Your feet seemed to be about a hand width smaller than my own." Sebastián shrugged. "And I was correct."

We sat in a circle and feasted on the bread, cheese, and fruit as Sebastián told us what he saw.

"There were guards everywhere. They were combing the village and stopping everyone. I myself was stopped thrice. They showed me your pictures and asked if I had any information. Of course, I said I did not. Unfortunately, we ran the opposite direction that we need to go when we escaped. I did find a way to the forest, but we should wait till dusk to make our way out. Otherwise we will be caught for certain."

I bit my lip. More disturbing news or, as Nana would say, I'd gotten myself into quite a pickle. Thinking about Nana would do me no good. I already missed her terribly and if I didn't make it to Geníru Castle by midnight, I'd never see her again. I'd never see any of my family again.

Olive gave my hand a squeeze. I looked over at her and she mouthed, "We'll make it."

Good, brave, and kind Olive always believed she could do anything. I just wished I had her faith.

Jeremey groaned. "So, we're stuck in this dusty building for the rest of the day? What are we going to do?"

"Someone will need to act as lookout in case the guards begin to search old buildings," Sebastián stated. "I suggest we take shifts. When it isn't your shift you should rest."

There was no way I was falling asleep again. I looked around and could see the others had the same thought as me.

"Why don't we clean this place up?" Olive suggested.

"Why? No one has been here in years and no one's bound to be here for years," Jeremey replied.

She shrugged. "You never know. Besides I was always taught you should leave a place better than you found it."

"I think it's a great idea," Nathan put in.

Jeremey rolled his eyes. "I'll take the first watch then."

∞ ∞ ∞

Olive and I discovered an old faucet in a back room that must have been a kitchen at one point. When we turned the faucet on, the water came out brown. After a few minutes, it cleared up. We rummaged around and found some old cloths that we used for dusting. The dust came off the floor in huge puffs, making us cough. Soon we were covered in it, looking as if we might be a gang of chimney sweeps.

Sebastian and Nathan climbed onto a rickety

table and began the task of cleaning the cobwebs off of the chandelier. The cobwebs seemed to stick to us as we danced around, trying to clean. About halfway through cleaning, Nathan switched out Jeremey as lookout and Jeremey grudgingly helped us. We found a disheveled mop in the kitchen. I went to stick the mop in water and Jeremey had a conniption fit.

"You can't just use water on floors like this." He pointed at the beautiful floor.

"Why?"

"It can ruin it!" he replied, rummaging through the cabinet.

"How do you know so much about wood floors?" I asked.

"His parents own a restoration business. He can talk about antique furniture for ages," Nathan said with a mock yawn from his post by the door.

Jeremey shot him a dark look and then pulled out wood floor cleaner that looked like it was from the eighties.

"Doesn't cleaner expire?" Olive said with trepidation.

Jeremey shrugged. "Maybe, but this will work much better than water."

"It'll also take longer," I replied.

"We've got lots of time," he said as he gathered more supplies to clean the floor.

I held back a groan as I followed him and Olive out of the small kitchen area.

∞ ∞ ∞

Several hours later, we surveyed our work with awe. The sunlight filtering through the windows caught the now-spotless chandelier at just the right angle, sending sparkles of light down on the brilliant hardwood floor. We had stacked the crates carefully in a corner and covered them back up with the long white cloth.

Olive had even taken the cloths we had used to clean and washed them out the best she could. She'd hung them to dry in the kitchen.

"If I wasn't so dirty, I'd feel like I was going to a ball." Olive laughed.

Nathan turned to her and bowed. "My lady."

She took his outstretched hand with a giggle and they began to waltz around the room. Nathan was surprisingly good. Jeremey lifted his arms and pretended to be playing an imaginary violin as he hummed a tune.

Sebastián came from the lookout station and bowed low to me. "Would you dance with me, Lady Rosie?"

"I suppose," I replied in a mock haughty tone.

He took my hands and led me through a dance that I wasn't sure existed anymore. I knew next to nothing about dancing as it was except for what I'd seen in movies, which wasn't much. After about the tenth time of stepping on his toes, we collapsed on the ground in laughter.

"After this is all over, you'll have to teach me more about dancing," I teased.

He nodded. "It would be my honor. It's only a pity I couldn't have my old dance instructor teach you."

Chapter 14

I was on lookout. The sun was setting and it was nearly time for me to wake everyone up. Nearly time for the final part of this crazy adventure to begin. I looked around the room at my friends. They were all still sleeping. I couldn't wake them up just yet. There was one thing I had to do first.

I carefully opened the front door. It didn't even make a squeak. I hurried through it and closed it just as carefully. The fresh night air hit my lungs and I took a deep breath in. How much better this air felt then the musty and dusty air of the old dance hall.

I stuck close to the building, making sure no one was about and no one would see me. The street was blessedly deserted. I took Olive's phone out of my pocket and turned it on. She'd not noticed when I grabbed it from her bag. With trembling fingers, I dialed the number that I had been forbidden to call for nearly a year.

It rang once, then twice, then…

"Rosie! Is that you?" Nana's sweet and beautiful voice came into my ear.

"Nana!" I choked out.

"Rosie, where are you? We've all been so worried. Your mom…"

"You're speaking to Mom?" I asked.

"Yes, she called me in a panic saying that you'd gone missing in Brussels. We're at the airport coming to find you. Where are you?"

I took a deep breath. "I just wanted to tell you I love you, Nana. Let Papa know I love him too and my family."

"Rosie, what has gotten into you?" Nana asked, her voice sounding worried. "Are you okay? I don't like the way you're talking. Whatever it is, let us help you."

Tears stung my eyes. Oh, how I wanted to be a little girl again and let Nana solve all my problems, but I couldn't.

"Promise me you'll tell them I love them." I begged. "And promise that you'll try and fix whatever happened between you and Mom."

Nana was silent for a moment. "I promise Rosie. I love you too."

A door opened down the street and I pressed myself close to the building.

"I've got to go Nana. I love you. Remember that," I said. "Goodbye."

I could hear her protests as I hung up the

phone. I felt the tears slide down my face as I turned the phone off once more and stuck it in my pocket. A slight noise behind me caused my heart to skitter, and I swung around only to find Sebastián in the doorway.

I felt like I'd been caught stealing a cookie from the cookie jar. Was he going to tell me I was foolish for calling my family? Did he even understand that was what I'd done?

He took both of my hands in his. "I understand. If I had the chance to tell my family goodbye, I would have."

I wrapped my arms around him in a hug and felt more tears fall down my face. "I'm sorry you never got to say goodbye."

He returned the hug and then pulled away. "It's in the past now and cannot be changed, but this doesn't have to be a goodbye to your family, Rosie. We still have a chance to fix this."

I nodded and we headed back into the dance hall to wake everyone up.

We walked down the road like thieves in the night, skirting the edges of streets and staying out of the lamplight. Sebastián held up his hand and we stopped dead in our tracks. In the distance, we could hear faraway conversation and then loud laughter. It faded away into the night and we continued on.

It felt as if we were truly going to battle, and the weight of the situation hung heavily on me. A few hours was all it would take to decide my fate. Would I live or would I die? It was dictated by an ancient curse that wasn't of my choosing. But did I choose it? I'd kissed a frog in a spur of the moment decision and the frog had turned out to be a cursed prince.

If I could take back the decision to kiss that frog, would I? I glanced at Sebastián ahead of me. He walked with the confidence of someone who knew what he wanted in life and he knew how to get it. I wouldn't take back that kiss. I would do it again even if I knew I'd be cursed to. Even though he could be incredibly annoying and had outdated opinions, I thought I was starting to love him. I wasn't sure if it was true love, but I wanted him to be a part of the rest of my life. I wanted to have a million different adventures with him—just not adventures where our lives were on the line.

I bumped into Olive, nearly toppling over. She pressed a finger to her lips as I struggled not to cry out. Sebastián was looking out around a corner. He reared his head back and ushered us behind a staircase. Footsteps and flashlight beams approached.

I held my breath, afraid to breathe too loudly. My heart pounded in my ears as the footsteps got closer and closer. Then they stopped and the flashlight beam hit a spot near my foot. I fought the urge to pull my foot in closer to me and Olive gripped my arm. After what felt like an eternity, the beam circled away from us and the footsteps continued the way we had come.

We all stood up silently, trying to not make a sound. We reached the corner once more. Sebastián looked out and then made a mad dash across the street. We followed. We turned one more corner and an old village gate came into view. It was open.

All caution gone, we ran toward it as fast as our legs would carry us. I'd never been a great runner but the adrenaline rushing through my veins pushed me faster than I'd ever gone. I was the first to make it through the gate. Sebastián caught up to me and grabbed my hand.

We ran until we reached the edge of the forest and then we skidded to a halt. I stared up at the large, imposing trees before us. Olive, Jeremey, and Nathan caught up to us and stared nervously into the forest as well.

"Here we go, into a haunted magical forest." Jeremey broke the silence. "It'll be as easy as eating pie, right?"

"If you hate pie, then yes," Olive responded.

My lips quirked in half a smile. "I hope it's easy. It's ten o'clock. We only have two hours."

"Well then, my fellow knights, what are we waiting for?" Jeremey called. "We have a fair maiden to rescue."

He marched into the forest, followed by the others.

I rolled my eyes. "How many times do I have to say it? I'm going to be the one doing the rescuing!"

I marched into the forest behind them. The mist of the forest swallowed us up and blocked the lights of the village from view. As we stumbled along, I tried to keep hoping. Hoping that we would be able to find our way to a castle. A castle that no one, not even the brightest historians, had been able to find. A place that had been lost to time for three hundred years. I wrapped my hand over the Ruby Amulet and let its warmth wash over me. It was all going to work out.

Chapter 15

I cried out as my knees hit the uneven forest floor. I heard a short rip and I knew that my favorite pair of jeans were ruined for good now. If all the dirt and the muck hadn't ruined them before, they now had a lovely large rip in the right knee.

"Are you well?" Sebastián asked with concern.

Olive pointed the flashlight at my knee. It had some lovely scrapes on it but it wasn't bleeding.

"I'm fine," I said, pushing myself up from the ground, ignoring the hand Sebastián offered.

That was the third time I'd tripped within the last half hour and the spot seemed eerily familiar.

"I think we're going in circles," I announced with trepidation. "That tree stump looks exactly the same as when I tripped the other two times."

Jeremey looked around nervously. "I can't

tell. Everything looks the same in here."

"We are continuing in the same direction," Sebastián said with confidence. "We cannot have passed this same stump twice."

"I'm positive," I replied. I could feel my anger rising. How much longer did we have? An hour to an hour and a half at best?

"How long since the last time you tripped?" Olive asked.

"Maybe ten minutes."

Olive took a pocket knife out of her bag and carved a quick line in the stump.

"Sorry," she told the stump, patting it.

"It can't hear you." Jeremey rolled his eyes.

"I've heard it's bad to carve into trees," Olive said as she stuffed the pocketknife back into her backpack. "Let's keep walking."

We all followed after Olive and her flashlight beam. I began to wish we had more than just one flashlight. I should have stuck to the packing list and brought one. Olive, ever vigilant, had been the only one to pack one for our trip. We weaved our way in and out of branches as we continued in the same direction. I tried to hold back a shiver. Nothing moved in this forest except us. There was no sound of animals moving and no branches blowing in the wind. It was simply silent. Even breathing seemed too loud for this place.

We skirted fallen tree limbs and hopped over forest streams. It hadn't felt very long at all before Olive stopped and shone her flashlight on a tree stump. There was one long mark in the stump. Exactly the same as Olive had just carved.

"I told you!" I glared.

I wasn't going to trip one more time on that thing. With my luck, the other knee of my jeans would rip. Not that it mattered anyway.

"How can this be?" Sebastián said, shaking his head. "I know the direction of my home. I was not leading us in a circle."

"We haven't been going in a circle," Olive confirmed. "But somehow we always end up right back here."

"It must be magic," I said. "No wonder no one has been able to find Geníru Castle."

We all fell silent. How were we to find a castle that was hidden by magic? I stared at the mark on the stump, willing it to have the answer.

Jeremey and Nathan started throwing out wild ideas.

"What if we walked backwards?"

"Maybe we need to figure out the magic spell that will make the way visible?"

I closed my eyes, trying to concentrate. How did one find a castle hidden by magic? With something else magic, maybe like a wand or...My eyes popped open. I reached for the Ruby Amulet still hanging from my neck. I removed it and held it up. I held it toward one direction. Nothing happened. I held it toward another. The amulet felt cold. I tried once more and the amulet began to faintly glow. I held my breath as I pointed it back in the direction I had just tried. The amulet's glow faded.

"It's like a game of hot and cold!" I exclaimed.

The others turned to stare at me.

"What are you talking about, Rosie?" Olive quirked an eyebrow.

"The amulet can lead us there. Look." I lifted the amulet in the correct direction. It glowed. When I moved it away, it stopped.

I turned back to the them, feeling giddy. Olive and Nathan were grinning while Sebastián and Jeremey looked hesitant to follow the Ruby Amulet anywhere.

"Let's go!" I told them, lifting the amulet in front of me, letting it guide our way.

It led us in zig zags around the forest and once it felt like we were going in a circle, but nothing looked familiar. The trees seemed to be wilder looking the further we went, as if no human had been in this part of the woods for three hundred years.

Twice, I made a wrong turn and the amulet's glow dimmed. Both times, I corrected my mistake and the amulet's light continued to grow until it looked like I was holding a fire ball in my hands.

"Isn't it burning you?" Jeremey asked, staring at the glowing amulet.

"No." In fact, the amulet only felt warm, not even hot.

I fought my way through a knot of trees and froze. I blinked, trying to wish away what was in front of us.

"It's just like from a fairytale," Olive whispered.

Towering at least thirty feet high was a wall covered in thorns. Thorns that were longer than my arm and nearly as thick as me.

"Maybe the amulet will burn through them?" Nathan suggested.

I walked carefully toward the wall of thorns, holding the amulet in front of me. I touched the amulet to one of the vines. For a moment it seemed as if the wall of thorns would snatch the amulet away from me. I pulled it away and hung it back around my neck.

"That won't work," I said, backing away from the wall.

Sebastián plopped his large hiking backpack on the ground, unzipped it, and pulled out a short sword.

He beamed. "This ought to do the trick."

He raced toward the wall of thorns and began hacking at it. Vines came down in chunks. We all jumped back as he expertly dodged the falling vines. He slashed at the thorns until a staircase was revealed. A staircase made of stone. It was then I realized the wall wasn't all thorns but the thorns had grown up a stone wall.

Sebastián smiled in satisfaction as he buckled his sword around his waist and picked up his backpack. "It looks like the gate was removed. What luck! I don't have a key."

"Where did you get that sword?" I asked.

"'Tis mine. I was wearing it when I was cursed."

"I didn't notice it when I broke the spell."

"It had fallen in the gardens. I went back for it."

"I'm glad you had it. We wouldn't have made it through those vines." Jeremey grinned.

"*Oui*, but we shall still need to be careful," Sebastián warned. "I may need to clear more vines before we make it to the top of the castle wall."

Without another word, he placed the backpack on his shoulders and raced up the stairs. Olive was the first to catch up to him, trying her best to shine the flashlight so he could see. After a few more hacks, we made it to the top of the wall.

"Well, dear friends, may I be the first to welcome you to Geníru Castle," Sebastián said solemnly as we looked out at his former home.

The castle looked trapped in time with its towering turrets and grand castle steps. It was made of a grey-white stone that shone in the moonlight, making it seem as if it were glittering.

A long and mournful toll filled the air. We all jumped. I nearly toppled into a thorn but Sebastián caught me. The toll sounded again.

"What is that?" Nathan said, covering his ears.

"'Tis our clock. Amazing it still works," Sebastián called over the tolls.

I held my breath and tried to count. How many tolls had it been? Ten? It stopped after I made it to eleven. I breathed a sigh of relief. We had an hour.

"I didn't know they had clocks that chimed three hundred years ago," Jeremey stated.

"Oh, the history of the clock is quite interesting, actually. There are some historical records that reference a clock chiming as early as the 1100's. Why, even..."

We all gave Olive a look.

"Right, this isn't the time," she said sheepishly. "If any of you do want to know about the history of clocks, you can ask me tomorrow."

I snorted, trying to cover my laughter. Olive playfully hit my arm.

"Come on." I grinned as I raced down the stairs into the castle courtyard.

Chapter 16

A s my foot hit the cobblestones of the courtyard, the world seemed to shift and tilt.
I nearly fell over once more. Sebastián
grabbed my arm, saving me from more bumps and
bruises.

"Did you feel that?" I asked the others.

They all nodded. Sebastian's face had drained
of color. I followed his gaze and my heart skipped a
beat. It was as if I was watching a movie filled with
characters from the 1700's. People milled about the
courtyard. There were woman tending stalls, children playing, and guards patrolling. I could hear the
chatter of their voices, but it was like a distant echo.
The images of the people seemed to flicker in and
out.

"Are they ghosts?" Olive said.

She waved at a little girl who was running
around the courtyard giggling. The child didn't see
her. Instead, she ran right through Olive and up the

stairs behind us. Olive jumped and cried out.

"Are you alright?" Nathan asked.

"It didn't feel like anything at all," Olive replied. "It just scared me."

Jeremey waved his hand through a passing guard. "If they are ghosts, they can't see us."

"They are not ghosts," Sebastián croaked. "They are a memory. This is what the courtyard looked like the day I took the Ruby Amulet. That little girl was the cook's daughter. The guard was my friend, William. I left at midday. Do you not see that the courtyard looks lighter than it should for being near midnight?"

Sebastián was right. We didn't need Olive's flashlight anymore. If I looked at the ground close enough, I could see past the memory of what the castle had looked like. The stones were dark and dirty, not light as the memory made them look.

"What is the quickest way to the throne room?" I asked, breaking through everyone's thoughts.

Sebastián straightened his shoulders and led the way through the courtyard. Ignoring the memories, he simply walked right through them. I tried to follow his lead but I couldn't get used to walking through people. I began to dodge in between them.

The front doors of the castle were wide open. Guards stood outside but they paid us no heed as we walked inside. My eyes had a hard time deciding what was a memory and what the castle actually looked like once we were inside.

Torches burned, lining the walls, but I knew those couldn't be real. Large tapestries hung with rich colors but every so often I would catch a waver in the memory and see the tapestry was in shreds.

Servants zoomed past us. A few maids were laughing in the corner over something a manservant said.

"Charlie always knew how to bring a laugh to someone's face," Sebastián said, staring at the servants. "I wonder what happened to him after I left?"

He didn't wait for a response but continued up a winding stairway. We followed him. As I stepped on one stair, a tile came loose and went tumbling down. I looked down at the stair. The memory of the tile was still there but the real tile was gone.

"We should be careful," I began. "The stairs aren't as stable as they—"

There was a loud rumbling and then stones began falling from above.

"Run!" I heard Nathan cry.

Sebastián grabbed my arm and hauled me up the rest of the stairs. We made it to the top and collapsed in a heap. I looked down the stairway. Most of it was now blocked with stones that had fallen from the ceiling. I could see the sky.

"Is everyone okay?" I asked, looking around.

My eyes met Sebastian's and I realized the others had been behind us. I hurried up from the ground and raced down the stairs to the pile of rubble.

"Olive?" I screamed. "Jeremey? Nathan, can you hear me?"

The memory of the castle was playing tricks on my eyes. It looked as if the staircase wasn't blocked. I could see down it but I couldn't see my friends.

"Are you alright?" I called again.

Several painful beats of my heart went by in silence. What had I done? I'd brought them into this mess and now they were buried in castle rubble.

One of the stones moved and clattered down by my foot. I hopped back.

"We're here," Olive cried, her dirty face visible through a small hole.

"Are you all alive? Is anyone hurt?"

"No, we're fine," she called back. "Just stuck on the other side. Is there another way up?"

"The servant's stairs," Sebastián told her.

The pile of stones gave an ominous groan.

"We'll find it. You two hurry to the throne room. We'll catch up," Olive called to us before her face disappeared.

"Be careful!" I yelled after her.

Sebastián and I raced back up the stairs. He took my hand as we ran down an ornate hallway. Halfway down, he skidded to a stop, staring at someone who stood by a window. A beautiful woman, perhaps in her late thirties, stared out the window. She had long golden hair that was braided intricately. A crown was woven into the braid.

"Is that your mother?"

Sebastián swallowed hard and nodded his head.

"She's beautiful," I told him.

He moved closer to the memory of his mother. "She would often stare out this window. I once asked her why. She told me she was dreaming of traveling to far off places like Marco Polo. She wanted to be an explorer and discover grand lands."

He raised his hand to touch her cheek but it went right through her. He dropped his hand with a defeated look.

"These memories haunt me. It nearly makes me wish I'd stayed a frog."

I grabbed his hand. "Don't. Perhaps your mother did travel after you left. Perhaps she did find grand places. And if she didn't, then you can find them for her."

"My father wasn't here the day I left," Sebastián said, looking away from his mother. "Not that I would want to see him. He wasn't known for being a caring father."

"Let's go, Sebastián," I said, tugging on his hand.

He looked back at his mother as if he might refuse to go and spend his last moments alive with her. Instead, he shook his head and turned away from her.

He walked with purpose down the hallway now. He ignored the rest of the memory people we passed. We came to a large door and he swung it open. The room had torches lit on either side as well with large stone thrones at one end. The thrones were embedded with jewels that sparkled in the firelight.

We paused in the middle of the room. An ornate sun mosaic was etched into the floor.

"Where does the Ruby Amulet go?"

Sebastián shook his head. "I know not. Katarina only said it had to be returned to the throne room."

I jumped as the clock began to toll. We were out of time. I tore the amulet from my neck and placed it gently in the middle of the mosaic. Nothing happened.

"Did it work?" Sebastián asked, but we both knew the answer.

We could still see the memory of torch light —something that wasn't really there.

Sebastián grabbed my hands. "I'm sorry, Rosie. I never meant for this to happen."

Then he kissed me. A short, sweet kiss. A kiss of goodbye.

"No!" I yelled, picking up the amulet. "We can't die. We're so close."

Sebastián gasped and fell to the ground. My vision began to spin and I felt as if I might fall as well.

The clock was still tolling.

I looked around the room, frantically searching for any place the amulet belonged. My eyes fell upon one of the thrones. At the top of it there was a hole. A place where a jewel should have been.

I stumbled toward it, nearly toppling over as I climbed the stairs. I pulled myself onto the throne and as the last toll sounded, pushed the amulet into the hole.

I slumped down into the throne, my vision darkening.

"Take it back, Katarina," I pleaded in a whisper.

There was a brilliant flash of light and I watched as the Ruby Amulet melded into the throne. Suddenly, the room darkened as the memory of torchlight extinguished. Instantly, it felt as if a heavy burden was lifted off of me and I could breathe.

"We did it, Sebastián. We did it!" I cried.

In the now only moonlit room, I noticed Sebastian's form still lying on the floor where he'd fallen. I raced down the stairs and to his side. I turned him over so I could see his face. He wasn't moving.

"Sebastián?" I whispered. "I broke the curse."

I shook him. "Sebastián, wake up! I did it. You're not supposed to die!"

Tears began falling from my eyes, splashing onto the mosaic below.

"Wake up, you silly prince. I love you!" I choked out

I bent down and kissed him. This was my kiss of goodbye. I'd broken the curse. Why had he died?

I broke the kiss and held back a sob. Sebastián gasped and his eyes flew open.

"You're alive!" I laughed in disbelief.

"You saved me."

I smiled and wiped away my tears. "I told you I would be the one rescuing you."

He grinned back at me and then pulled my face toward his for another kiss. This was my happily ever after.

Epilogue

I could see reporters crowded around the barricade that was put up to block their entrance. Sebastián, Rosie, Jeremey, Nathan, and I sat waiting in the courtyard as police peppered us with questions. Why did we sneak out? How did we know where to look? If so, why didn't we just tell the authorities?

We didn't have great answers. We hadn't planned to be found when we were still at the castle. After the curse had been broken, Sebastián and I had found the others. Without the light of the memory torches, I would have been lost until morning without Sebastian's help. When we had found them, we decided to wait until morning to head back out into the forest. At the first light of dawn, Nathan had noticed the wall of thorns that had surrounded the castle was gone.

Soon after, we heard voices calling our names from the forest. When the police officers found us in a long-lost castle, their eyes nearly popped out of their heads.

"It's the find of the century," one said in awe.

After another barrage of questions, Olive spoke up.

"It was my idea," she began. "I've been obsessed with Geníru for a few years. I thought I knew where the castle was and if I'd told anyone where I thought it was, they wouldn't have believed me."

"So, I told her we had to find it ourselves," I jumped in. "And then Jeremey and Nathan overheard our plans and wanted to come."

The officer scratched his head and looked at Sebastián. "And where do you fit in… what was your name…ah, Sebastián Gene?"

I bit my lip. Sebastián's real last name was Geníru. He'd begun to tell the officers but I'd cut him off and said it was Gene.

"We met him near Brussels. His dad used to be an archeologist so Sebastián offered to help us find the castle," I supplied.

The officer raised his eyebrows. "And your parents have no working telephone?"

"Pardon me, officer," a melodic voice cut in.

"Mother?" Sebastián's mouth fell open.

I turned to stare at the woman who had spoken. Gone was the regal hairstyle, crown, and flowing dress, but there was no denying that it was his mother. Her modern-day style was classy, reminding me a bit of Audrey Hepburn with her hair swept into a ponytail.

"This is your son?" he asked.

"Yes, Sebastián Gene," she replied. "We live in Brussels. We just moved there and I've not had time to get a telephone installed."

The officer looked charmed and in awe of her. He struggled to find something to say.

"Would you mind if I talk to my son?" she asked, beaming at the officer.

The officer ran a hand through his thinning hair. "Please do. I've got a mountain of paperwork to start."

She placed a hand on the officer's arm. "I must apologize for my son. He's caused a lot of trouble for all of us."

"No apologies needed, ma'am," the officer said.

"Thank you."

The officer nodded, looking as if all sense had left him. He turned and walked away, leaving us to stare at Sebastián's mother.

"Sebastián, where are your manners? Aren't you going to introduce me to your friends?" she asked.

When he made no move to respond, she beamed at us. "My name is Ivy Gene."

"How are you still alive?" Sebastián sputtered, tears filling his eyes.

She smiled and cupped his face in her hands. "Katarina could see the future. She knew before you were born what you would do. From the moment you turned into a frog, the spell Katarina gave me started to work. I didn't begin to age again until you became human once more."

"But...how?"

"Even if people no longer believe in magic that doesn't mean it no longer exists." She smiled and placed a kiss on his forehead, then she turned to me. "And you must be the girl with golden curls who rescued my son and Geníru?"

"I guess," I told her. I could feel myself blushing.

"And a band of worthy knights?" she said, glancing at Olive, Jeremey, and Nathan.

They nodded. Olive seemed too awestruck to speak. I could just imagine what was going through her head. Here was an actual queen from the eighteenth century. She could learn so much about history from her.

"I thank all of you from the bottom of my heart." She then stared around. "How wonderful it is to see this place again. I think I'll take a walk around. Walk with me, dear."

Sebastián nodded and followed his mother as they walked around the courtyard.

"This day is getting crazier and crazier." Jeremey broke the silence.

We all nodded in agreement.

"How mad do you think my parents will be?" Nathan asked.

"Knowing your parents, you'll probably be grounded till you're thirty," Jeremey responded.

"It was worth it," Nathan said, looking at

Olive.

Olive noticed and blushed.

"Et tu Nathan?" Jeremey asked in mock shock.

Nathan and Olive blushed in unison and we all laughed.

"Maybe there is some cursed princess you could rescue," Nathan suggested. "Sebastián can't be the only cursed royalty out there."

"It's true. There are dozens of stories of princes and princesses disappearing mysteriously," Olive put in.

"I am pretty good at helping people break curses." Jeremey laughed.

"It does make me wonder how many other frogs are actually cursed people?" Olive began.

"Perhaps we should start a curse-breaking business?" Jeremey said. "We could call it The Curse Breakers."

"Let's do it!" Nathan beamed. "But let's change the name. The Curse Breakers is lame."

"If that is what you would truly like to do, I have quite a lot of research I could give you," Sebastian's mother said as they rejoined us. "I spent a hundred years doing research on magical curses. I've even helped break a few curses in my time."

I didn't have time to process what she said because at that moment, someone screamed my name. I looked toward the sound and saw Nana...my Nana, running toward me. I could see Papa and my parents behind her but she was far outpacing them.

I rushed toward her. Time seemed to stand still as we met and she enfolded me in her arms.

"Oh, my girl, am I glad to see you." She held me back, surveying my face. "What happened? Tell me everything and not that silly story you told the police. I know how to spot a lie from a mile away."

"You wouldn't believe me if I told you the truth." I smiled.

"I very much doubt that. What have I always told you about this part of the world?" she asked, not waiting for an answer. "It's a place of magic."

My smile widened. "A place where a girl can kiss a frog and he turns into a prince."

"How do you think I met your grandfather? I met him under a lamp post but that doesn't mean he was human when I met him."

"Hello, Lottie," Ivy broke in.

Nana smiled. "I knew you would be here, Ivy. I'm so happy you've found your son at last."

"Your granddaughter was a big help." Ivy smiled.

I blinked, my brain trying to process everything that was happening. I shook my head and I opened my mouth to tell Nana everything, but at that moment, I was bear-hugged by my parents and grandfather. I let them hug me. My story could wait. Perhaps I would never be able to tell my parents what had happened, but Nana and Papa would believe.

Acknowledgement

Thank you to my family who are my biggest fans. Thank you for helping me to stay motivated to keep writing. They truly are my favorite people on this planet. I'm so blessed to have them.

Thank you to my dear friend Kayla for being obsessed with frogs. Her obsession helped inspire this story. Thank you to Krista for doing the cover design. It's gorgeous and I love it!!! Thank you, Jayden, for being a model.

A big thanks to my editor Jeigh Meredith with Salt and Sage books. This story would not be what it is without you. Andrea, thank you for reading my book and giving me feedback. Only a true friend would read your book while they are in labor.

I'm grateful to my Heavenly Father for giving me a love of writing and storytelling. And lastly dear reader I'm grateful for you. Thank you!

About The Author

Ashley I. Hansen

Ashley I. Hansen grew up in a small Northern Utah town surrounded by mountains. She's always had a wild imagination, a passion for history, and a love for a good story. When she isn't writing you can usually find her curled up with a good book, exploring the beautiful mountains of Utah, or eating chocolate.

Books By This Author

Thaw

Eira knew the moment the arrow struck true she would be banished from her village. Banishment on the Ice meant certain death, but an ancient secret could save her life. With nothing left to lose Eira sets out for a kingdom, she thought only existed in legend. After finding the kingdom she realizes it's nothing like the legends told.

Prince Aric wasn't born to be a king, but he finds himself next in line to the throne. He wants it even less after he fishes Eira out of the Eis Sea. As Aric tries to secure a political alliance through marriage the threat of war overshadows the kingdom. Endeavoring to discover fact from fiction in political intrigue Aric unearths a secret that will change not only his life but the fate of the kingdom forever.

See author's Amazon page for more details!